Born in Bellevue, Washington, USA, Jonah Quinn Barenboym is a phenomenal writer of short stories and novels in the sci-fi genre. He's been writing since the age of 14 and his stories are fast-paced and captivating. *The Dreams That Hold Us Captive* is Jonah's publishing debut, which follows the protagonists Noah and Theo through thrilling twists and turns as they aim to free the world of a dark and evil force. Jonah Quinn currently resides in London, UK and enjoys gaming when he's not writing while also pursuing his studies.

Jonah Quinn Barenboym

THE DREAMS THAT HOLD US CAPTIVE

AUSTIN MACAULEY PUBLISHERS
LONDON · CAMBRIDGE · NEW YORK · SHARJAH

Copyright © Jonah Quinn Barenboym 2025

The right of Jonah Quinn Barenboym to be identified as author of this work has been asserted by the author in accordance with sections 77 and 78 of the Copyright, Designs and Patents Act 1988.

All rights reserved. No part of this publication may be reproduced, stored in a retrieval system, or transmitted in any form or by any means, electronic, mechanical, photocopying, recording, or otherwise, without the prior permission of the publishers.

Any person who commits any unauthorized act in relation to this publication may be liable to criminal prosecution and civil claims for damages.

This is a work of fiction. Names, characters, businesses, places, events, locales, and incidents are either the products of the author's imagination or used in a fictitious manner. Any resemblance to actual persons, living or dead, or actual events is purely coincidental.

A CIP catalogue record for this title is available from the British Library.

ISBN 9781035885268 (Paperback)
ISBN 9781035885275 (ePub e-book)

www.austinmacauley.com

First Published 2025
Austin Macauley Publishers Ltd®
1 Canada Square
Canary Wharf
London
E14 5AA

I would like to thank my dad, Ruslan Barenboym, for his undying encouragement and support throughout the developing, writing, and publication of this book.

Chapter 1

"No matter how much I scrub, I'll never be clean…" Theo muttered, aggressively washing his hands as he had been for a few minutes already.

"Theo! Get your obsessive ass down here! You're gonna miss the game!" Noah exclaimed. "Your hands are fine!"

Theo sighed as he dropped his head. He turned off the faucet and dried his hands on the towel, then stepped out of the bathroom and moped his way downstairs. Noah sat on the couch , impatiently waiting for Theo to come to watch the soccer match. He patted the spot next to him, inviting Theo to take a seat.

"So who's playing?" Theo asked, though he took no interest in this match or soccer in general.

"Tonga versus Somalia! This is gonna be so exciting…"

Theo rolled his eyes and sat down next to his brother, realizing there was nothing better to do that evening than to join him and watch the game. He struggled to stay awake. He was bored out of his mind.

"Dude, they're like, the world's worst teams ever." Theo yawned. "How can you even watch them for, like, so long, man?"

Theo's head drooped down. His eyelids were heavy.

"What? You think this is boring?" replied Noah.

Theo subtly nodded, his eyes already closed, and before he knew it, he had fallen asleep. Noah rolled his eyes and fixed his gaze on the TV screen.

"*Gooooooooaaaaaaal!*" Noah shouted, startling Theo.

With his eyes half open, Theo stood up and left the living room. He slowly made his way upstairs, where Noah's screams would become softer and resting would be easier. He jumped into bed and hid under the covers, feeling cozy. However, Noah's excitement would still ruin the silence. He didn't mind anymore that Theo wasn't there to watch with him.

"Just ignore it… go to sleep…"

"So, what'd you dream about?" Noah asked, sitting beside him with a notepad and pencil in hand.

Theo slowly opened his eyes, tired and groggy.

Familiar with the routine, Theo glared at Noah and responded, "I'll never understand this weird hobby of yours… Anyway, I dreamt about this thing…"

Intrigued, Noah enquired, "Well? What was it?"

"It was a big soccer ball! And it was so boring! It just rolled around the city in circles and did nothing."

Noah's face went dull as he noted down Theo's dream description.

"Of course," he muttered under his breath. "Why would I ever expect anything more?" He finished writing about the dream and stood up. "Alright then, Theo. You have a very interesting mind," Noah remarked sarcastically.

He left the room, ready to start his next masterpiece.

Noah had a peculiar interest in creating art inspired by his own dreams, as well as the dreams of anyone kind enough to share theirs. Every morning, Noah would finish his routine with a detailed sketch from his mind, though sometimes they could look quite abstract. Later, he would take Theo's dreams from his afternoon naps and draw those too. Some of the artwork he particularly liked, he would paint. All around Noah's room hung framed paintings of his favorite dreams, drawings and ideas. This schedule would repeat every day, over and over again, until one day, Noah received an idea from Theo that was somewhat unexpected. His face lit up as he leaned forward, preparing to take some exciting notes.

Theo whimpered. "It was… horrible… They grabbed me and threw me in a room. It was so small and cramped, and the door was made of iron bars. I was scared…"

Noah wrote it all down with interest. "Like a prison cell? Were you arrested for something?"

"Oh, it was… It was some kind of prison cell. But no, I didn't do anything wrong," continued Theo, visibly disturbed by his dream. "I couldn't speak. It happened so fast, there was nothing to say. I could hardly c-c-omm—"

"Comprehend?"

"Yes, comprehend what was happening to me. And though I was afraid, I could see the sky through my cell door… It was beautiful. There was pink, purple, orange, and all the cool colors mixed together and it was really pretty."

Noah showed even more excitement as he completed the notes and flipped the page of his notepad.

"So, anything else?"

"Yeah. There were five people flying in the air, with these cool masks on their faces. I think they were in charge or something."

Noah noted down the final details. "Thanks a lot, Theo! This will be a special one."

Theo nodded, though his face still showed worry. A strange dream indeed, hopefully never to be seen again.

Two Hours Later

Theo walked downstairs, now feeling refreshed. As he glanced to the side, he saw his brother painting in the art room. Theo entered to take a closer look. The painting perfectly matched his dream description. It was—disturbing, to say the least—yet mesmerizing. The colors of the sky blended beautifully together, replicating a purple sky with orange highlights and pink mixed in. The landscape was covered by the prison's cell lines and reinforced walls. And right in the middle of the picture, the canvas was blank—incomplete. Noah had left an outline of five mysterious figures, not knowing what they would've looked like. He drew a question mark on each of them, then stepped back to admire his painting. He was speechless.

"For once, you actually made a pretty decent piece of art," Theo mocked.

"I'll take it. This is definitely one of my favorites. I don't know what you did to finally dream something interesting, but please do it again," Noah replied with a chuckle. "Ah, I'm totally framing this. I'm putting it in the center of my room, where it'll stand out from all the others."

"I think I see why you like doing this now… It's infinite inspiration, and the ideas are so… special. They actually make your drawings and paintings interesting. At least this one is."

"See? I'm not weird for doing this. You finally understand."

"Actually, you are still weird for doing this, but now I see where you're coming from."

"Alright, fair enough. Now let's just wait for this to dry, and I'll take it up later."

"Alright then," replied Theo, as he followed behind Noah.

He paused for a moment and looked back at the painting. The talent was truly admirable. He turned back and left the room.

Later, Noah thought for a moment. He lay still in bed, pondering Theo's odd dream. He wondered what could transpire next, whether in his dream or Theo's. He hoped Theo would be alright and that he wouldn't dream of something horrible again.

Suddenly, Noah found himself in a small room. It was almost empty, except for the tilted paintings on each wall. The walls were white and stained with mould and fungus. Something unknown, hidden behind the walls, emitted a stench. The room left an uncanny vibe.

Noah slowly walked forward, but he noticed the paintings started to fade in color. The closer Noah came, the less vivid each painting seemed. Noah walked towards one. As he stood in front of it, there was nothing visible but a frame and a blank canvas. All the paintings around the room had turned the same, except for one. A feeling of unease, confusion and curiosity filled Noah as he walked towards the picture.

Deepcity

The caption of the frame read. The title accurately presented the artwork. It was overwhelming. Roads covered the land leading in every direction, with even more built up in layers. The buildings were quite crammed and compact, with the appearance of three different shops in the same window. There was so much, in fact, that the buildings were not the correct height to scrape the sky but to tower over it. The sky was covered by architecture blocking almost every angle. From what *was* seen up above, smog filled the air around, turning the sky into a polluted, gray, gloomy one.

Before Noah got to look at the detailed painting any longer, Theo emerged, straightening all the pictures on the wall with a look of frustration on his face.

"You hang up all these pictures, and you just leave them tilting. One job, people!"

Theo came up to the *Deepcity* picture and tilted it straight. "That's much bett—"

Theo was interrupted by the loud noise of complex mechanisms working behind the walls. Gears turned, motors ran, and a chunk of the wall started to budge. The boys perked up at it. The wall glided further back, revealing a secret stairway. Though it was hard to tell, with no illumination there and dust particles filling the air.

"Wow, your OCD finally did something useful for once—"

But Noah's speech was cut off by his massive coughing fit. They both seemed to be coughing non-stop, and smoky dust blew in their eyes. The world was going black; everything was fading out slowly. Suddenly, it was quiet.

Noah rolled over and kicked the blankets off in an attempt to cool off. Several seconds later, it was too cold without them. Then Noah opened his eyes. *That was… interesting,* he thought.

Later, Noah was enjoying his fruit bowl for breakfast. It consisted of sliced bananas, apples, berries and more fruits, all covered in honey and chia seeds. All of a sudden, Theo came running down the stairs in tears to exclaim something incredibly important.

"*Last night, I dreamt that they pum-0-m-ennnn* thh-h-h… And *then—*"

His words came rapidly, like a rapper's and were completely incomprehensible. Tears rolled down his cheeks as he sobbed like a child, with snot running down his nose.

"Wait, I can't understand a word you're saying! Slow down. Deep breaths, deep breaths." Theo took a deep breath and tried again.

"S-so basically, they trpp'd mnn thh cjjjjhe—" he tried before bursting into tears once again.

"What?"

"The *prison!* I went back!" Theo let out a devastating wail and buried his face in Noah's shoulder.

Noah wrapped his arms around him and patted him on the back.

"There, there…"

He comforted him, confused.

Sniffling, Theo managed to get a few more words out. "It was… more clear now… I saw their clothes and their m-masks," he stated, trembling in shock. "They were th-th-e same, no, not the same, b-but kinda similar, plain black with a white eye in the middle! It looked c-cool, but I was scared."

"Okay. We're seeing your therapist about this today. I'm sorry that happened, but you can't keep overreacting over a dream. Go get dressed."

Theo obeyed and walked back upstairs, still trembling, sniffling, and wiping away his tears.

Chapter 2

"So... let me get this straight. You first had a dream about going to prison, and then you had the same dream again. Apparently you were sobbing, overreacting and had to come here to talk about it?"

"Yeah, that's right... but—but you would be afraid too if you had that same dream! Let alone twice!"

"Well, I'm not here to tell you that it's unacceptable, especially considering..."

Noah waited outside, trying to listen to what the therapist had to say. He put his ear to the door, stealthily moving so as to not reveal that he was eavesdropping, and listened closely. He mostly heard the voice of the therapist talking; no responses from Theo. He must have been too scared to reply. Though Noah pressed his head against the door, it was unclear what the therapist was saying. The therapist's speech sounded muffled, practically inaudible.

Suddenly, Noah sprung back as he heard footsteps coming towards the door. He made it to his seat in the nick of time.

"You guys were right," Theo announced with a brave and serious face. "It's just a dream! I'm not gonna be scared anymore. I'm not a baby; I can handle a scary dream. I don't care if the same dream comes a third time! I'm an adult! Come at me!"

Noah gave him an awkward stare. "Well, at least it seems you're feeling better about this…"

"You'll see! I won't be afraid."

"Alright then," he replied, standing up from the seat. "Let's go home…"

As the two walked down the hall to leave, Noah couldn't help but notice a sense of worry behind Theo's display of courage. Whatever he was dreaming about, it truly got to him. Therapy couldn't help this. All of a sudden, Theo caught him staring.

"What?"

"Nothing, nothing…" Noah shifted his head forward and kept on walking.

He couldn't dodge the thought. It seemed to be more than a scary dream. It was repeating. Whatever the dream was, it made a grown man cry. Later that day, Noah still couldn't stop thinking about it. Theo stayed quiet and kept his head down; his fear gradually became more apparent. It was clear now that his mental state was deprecating, and this situation was a significant matter.

Later that day, the sun had set and it was time to return. It was time to sleep. Time to see if Theo could handle another dream well or if he would overreact again.

Noah thought, *If Theo freaks out over that dream again, I don't know what I'll do.*

Soon, Noah was falling asleep too.

He could hear muffled communication. Two people on either side of him tightly grasped his arms. They had iron grips; it was impossible to escape. As Noah's eyes grew wider, he could see that he was being taken to what looked like a prison cell. Suddenly, he was thrown in, and the door slammed shut and locked. Noah sprung up to his feet and held the metal bars, looking out with eyes filled with emotion. He was confused. Afraid. Angry. He shook the bars of the door, but it wouldn't budge. It was no use; he was imprisoned in his own dream. Outside his cell, he could see many others looking exactly the same. Although this wasn't a regular prison, the cell blocks were shaped in a horseshoe layout, and it was outdoors. From below, the violet sky was noticeable, while five humanoid figures appeared in the distance. They looked like people levitating. They wore these masks, hiding their entire faces. Their heads were covered with hoods or hats. Their clothes varied in style. Albeit a bit challenging to see them from a distance, he could infer that they were the place's wardens. One of them wore a mask different from the others'. Instead of having a white eye in the middle, it had white, triangular teeth. It looked psychotic.

Noah peered back down and saw the gate he had been dragged through, with tall, masked men standing on either side of it. In sync, they looked at their wrist watches and immediately at Noah. He felt a shiver down his spine, wondering what it could mean. He felt goosebumps emerge. He was worried, until… he woke up.

Noah jerked up, sitting straight in his bed. He couldn't comprehend what just happened—that he had the same dream as Theo's. He could now see why he was so concerned. But Noah's worry quickly went away, as he knew it was just a dream. Theo acted like a child; he couldn't handle uncomfortable dreams like an adult could.

Noah's concern returned. This wasn't just a dream. It was a recurring one, and somehow, the way it appeared, contagious. Noah decided to check on Theo to see if he had the same dream again, and if he did, how he felt afterwards.

Noah knocked on his door softly, hoping to see Theo awake, refreshed, and happy.

"Come in," Theo called after sighing.

Noah walked in to see Theo sitting on the edge of his bed, staring at the floor with a blank face. His expression was ambiguous; it was difficult to tell whether he was feeling fine or afraid. With exhaustion in his eyes, he looked up at Noah. Theo almost looked depressed.

"I had the dream again…" he stated. "But I've been thinking about it all. I know it's just a dream. Not to say it doesn't bother me anymore, but I'm not overreacting again. That's a good sign, right?"

"Well yeah, but—"

"The thing that *does* bother me though is the fact that I'm having this same freaky dream over and over again. Not even that, but it's slightly different every night. Almost as if it's really happening. Do you know what that feels like?" Theo asked, looking Noah dead in the eyes.

"I- uh… I guess not. But I wanted to tell you, I had that dream last night too. I see now why you were so afraid. Whatever's going on, it's not just a bad dream. I don't know if it's some brotherly psychology or something, but your dreams seem to be contagious to me."

"It really feels real. I think it will go away eventually. You know what they say—time heals everything. Right?"

Knowing there was nothing else that could be done, Noah sighed.

"Yeah, I guess so…"

Throughout the day, the boys didn't talk much. They held on to their thoughts as their minds lashed against themselves. Noah made sandwiches for lunch. He sat across from Theo and stared at him. Theo sat there, just staring at his food. He didn't seem hungry; everything going on in his head must have distracted him from an appetite.

"You know…" Noah spoke, finally breaking the silence. Theo didn't look up. "Before I had the dream with… the prison and all, I dreamt of this room full of paintings. All of them were blank except one. It was a painting of some steampunk-looking city, with tall buildings and a polluted sky. On the frame, the painting seemed to be titled *Deepcity*. Was that it? It's hard to remember now, but anyway—"

Theo's ears perked up upon hearing this information.

"*Deepcity?*" Theo interrupted. "You know those five people in power? From my short experience, I learnt some things. They call themselves the Dreamers, and the leader, the one with the different mask, is named Magnus. Who knows if it's his real name? One time, I overheard him talking about a dream he once had. It was just like you described. He called it *Deepcity* because of how crowded everything was. He felt like it was another level of urban life, deep within the wonders of a city looking like that."

"Very interesting," Noah replied.

With that, Theo took his first bite of the sandwich and continued to stay silent like a mouse. His chewing was inaudible, with his small nibbles. It was distinct, through his pale face and traumatized eyes, that countless thoughts continuously raced through his head. Clearly, a lot to handle. Noah observed and began eating too. At this point, he felt even more sympathy for Theo as he began to face the same feelings.

Chapter 3

The violet sky once again shone brightly above the prison. Noah woke up and immediately noticed where he was. He leapt up from the paved ground and grasped the bars, frantically looking beyond them and around the place.

"No!" Noah slammed his fist against the sonorous metal bars. "I can't be here! Not again!" he exclaimed, continuing to bash his hand on the cell door.

It rang beautifully and quite loudly. Loud enough, in fact, that it caught the attention of five lanky masked people levitating in the air. As he slowly glided down closer to the horseshoe, Noah felt butterflies race around in his stomach like never before.

Shit, shit, shit! he thought, jumping back to press himself flat against the inside wall of his cell.

"Attention prisoners! You may not know why you're all here, but I assure you, there is a reason for that. You don't have to worry about a single thing. My name is Magnus, and I built this entire place. My fellow helpers and I made *sure* that this place is inescapable. So guess what? You might as well get used to this now!" Magnus let out a sick, villainous laugh—which almost sounded fake—and continued to address his victims. "Because the more you complain, try to escape or *whatever*, we'll just make your stay even longer!" With that, Magnus let out another despicable cackle, and he and the Dreamers levitated away.

"Jesus, that laugh is annoying. I'm sure there's *some* way I can escape."

Magnus, who had just somehow appeared in front of the cell, stood tall and gave Noah a deadly stare as Noah scanned around for anything that could possibly help him. When Noah saw this, he jumped like a cat frightened at the sight of a cucumber. Goosebumps appeared all over his skin, and his eyes grew wide with shock.

"Did I stutter? I said *no one* leaves this place. Just remember. I can do *anything* to you. Shall I demonstrate?"

Paralyzed with fear, Noah couldn't even respond. He shivered in horror. He trembled in fear. He stared at Magnus with petrified eyes. Unable to shake his head or respond with a simple 'no', he only waited for Magnus' next move.

"Okay then. Don't let me hear that from you, *or anyone*," Magnus projected, turning around, pointing to the rest of the poor victims in their cells. "Who doesn't want their stay to be any more *miserable* than it should be!"

And with that, Magnus vanished in the blink of an eye.

After a few minutes, Noah seemed to calm down. He sat cross-legged in his cell, trying to comprehend.

I'm in a dream, he thought. *I know I am. So then why can't I just… wake up? Come on. Wake up! Wake up! Wake up…* He lightly hit his forehead in frustration before trying again. *Come on! Wake up! Do I not have control over my own mind anymore?*

He continued to shake his head with his eyes shut in an attempt to escape the horrors of the prison. He punched himself. Pinched himself. Scratched himself. No matter what he tried, he was truly stuck. His mind was truly under control. Suddenly, he stood up and kicked the cell door.

"Bullshit!" He punched the door. "Bullshit! Bullshit! Bullshit!" Noah exclaimed, repeatedly punching the unbreakable bars. "Fuck this!" He cried after vainly landing his final blow.

People in their own cages started to peer up at Noah. Collecting himself, he noticed the strange looks he was getting, and his face turned slightly red. Suddenly, a voice reverberated through the cell block, rivalling the other whispers, mutters and shouts of close innocents.

"Yeah! We don't deserve to be here!"

Curious, Noah looked in the direction of the sound, but they were too far away. He sighed as he fell back against the wall of his cell, sliding down to sit on the floor. Noah rested his face on his knees. He moaned and groaned. Soon, he began to sob.

...Why?

Noah woke up in a cold sweat and sprung up in bed, pale and distraught. *This is really getting out of hand! Seriously...* Hyperventilating, he wiped his forehead and slowly crawled out of bed. *Normally, I would be fine. It's just a dream; I'm awake now. I'd usually be able to get over it. But no... This is different. I... I need to calm down...*

And so he came, sulking out of his room, down the stairs to have breakfast. This would consist of an apple and two cups of coffee. Noah typically ate this way when he felt stressed or extremely tired in the morning. Today, it was both. Maybe three cups?

Noah suddenly tripped on the stairs, almost stumbling down had he not caught himself on the rail. He quickly shook his head for a moment, then continued to make his way down and towards the kitchen. Eventually, he arrived. He stood in place, processing his decision on what to eat. He turned his head slightly to stare at the coffee machine. After a few seconds, Noah snapped back to reality, blinked a few times, and walked over to open a cabinet containing cups and mugs. He grabbed three mugs at once, set them on the counter, and reached further back to take a much bigger mug—at least four times the size of the normal-sized ones—and placed it on the counter. Then he returned the three other mugs and closed the cabinet. This mug was never often used; it only sat in the back of the cupboard, collecting dust and acting as a nice decoration. Noah was never sure why he had bought it; perhaps one day he would gain some strong craving for one giant, dark, strong espresso.

Noah waited as the oversized mug started filling with coffee. He was unsure whether the machine even held enough.

"You're gonna drink that whole thing?" Theo asked with wide eyes.

Upon hearing this, Noah jumped up and yelped, goosebumps and hair standing up, frightened at Theo's unexpected presence.

"Jesus! When did you get here? You almost gave me a heart attack…" Noah grinned and chuckled, reacting to his own reaction.

"Are you okay? Did the dream get to you again?"

Noah nodded, subtly showing a look of sorrow on his face.

"Yeah... and you?"

"You know it," replied Theo. "But I'm used to it now. After all, they can't hurt us in real life."

"Let's hope."

Noah glanced back at his coffee, filled about halfway now. Theo walked over to the living room and turned on the TV. After a brief second, the news channel loaded.

"...are outraged by this insane phenomenon. Now we have a special guest, Timor.

Tell us, Timor, what was your first experience like in this devastating penitentiary of a dream?

How are you holding up?"

Intrigued, Theo leaned closer to the TV. It seemed they were talking about the dream prison. *Everyone* was going through the same thing.

"Hey Noah! Come over here!"

Curious, Noah rushed to the living room. The words *dream prison* were instantly understood as he heard them.

"It... it was horrible! I was only truly scared the second time, because that's how I knew this was a recurring dream! I thought I was going insane. And I wanted to try escaping, but I couldn't gather the courage to do it. I just waited in my cell, sobbing. And get this! Every time Magnus saw someone so upset, he would summon some whip in his hand—don't ask me how—and he would hit them as hard as he could! Even though it's in a dream, it hurts like hell!"

Noah and Theo looked at each other with an expression of *Yeah, we're victims too, but this is seriously concerning*. They kept staring at the TV. Noah was so immersed that he didn't hear the coffee machine play the finishing beeps.

"Well, that is certainly something! The crazy part is, it's something most of us, if not all of us, can relate to! Timor, how long do you think you can live with this?"

"Not gonna lie to you, I've been thinking a lot lately about ending it all..."

"Woah there! We don't need to be speaking of that here right now. Anyway, as..."

Noah thought for a moment.

"Do you know what this means?"

"Uh, that we're not the only ones going through this?"

"Well, no shit, Theo! It means that, say, if everyone on Earth experienced this, it could be the end of the world as we know it. This might be the start of an apocalypse!"

Theo stared blankly at Noah, then stared down in thought.

"Maybe you're right. Everyone will lose their minds over these recurring dreams. Man, this is serious. How will it all end?"

"Perhaps we'll all die," Noah replied with a shrug. "If it really is an apocalypse, everyone will be violent. Everyone will overdose on drugs to keep their minds distracted. And just like the guy on TV said, many will kill themselves to escape the misery. And to be honest, I don't blame them."

"No, no, no... Not like this. Even if it's the most realistic outcome, I don't want it to end this way! I say we need a leader. Someone who's brave enough to stand up against the

Dreamers' authority and start a rebellion. Someone who can look Magnus in the eyes and tell him, '*I'm not afraid*'."

"Uh-huh. And how will *that* work out? No one has power like him. As long as we come back to the same place every night, he's unstoppable. He's in our heads. Just wait till he messes with us in real time. Remember, he's a real person, too. He's behind this all, and the only way to stop him is to catch him in real life."

Noah realized the potential of the solution he just explained. His and Theo's eyes grew with excitement.

"Dude, that's it!" Theo exclaimed. "Remember that dream you had with the paintings?"

"You got into Magnus' head!" Theo grabbed Noah's shoulders and shook him back and forth.

"*You* can figure out who he is! You're like, the key to all this!"

"Oh my God, you're right! *Deepcity* was Magnus' dream, right? And I saw it in a painting."

"What if I have another dream like that one again? What if I see a painting of his house? His face?"

"The flag of the country he lives in?"

"It's not a bad idea. We just have to wait until you get one of those dreams again. We could stop this all!"

Chapter 4

Two Weeks Later

"Alright, we're here," Noah said after parking the car against the outer wall.

The boys left the vehicle and walked up to the double doors of the small building. Above the doors was a neon sign with flickering letters. Most of the words had burnt out, rendering them challenging to read in the darkness of the night. Inside the building were many old men, drinking, flirting, getting slapped by the women they tried to flirt with, and others playing pool. It was a bar. Some men sat at the counter with their heads down in their arms, whining to the bartender about the troubles they experienced with their dreams too.

Noah and Theo walked in. The bell at the door's top rang.

"You two dreaming it too?" spoke the bartender.

The boys realized that the bartender was addressing them. They looked at each other and then back at the bartender. They slowly nodded.

"Yeeeah, so does everyone else here. Come and take a seat," his voice was casual. Calm.

"Why's it so crowded today?" Noah asked.

"Everyone came for the same reason you did. Sometimes, drinking away your problems is a pretty easy way out of thinking about it all."

"Ah, I figured. Anyway, can we get two pints?"

"The usual?"

"Yeah, the usual…"

"Comin' right up."

Theo looked around, observing the wild animals this place held. It was obnoxious, though no one started any fights.

"Dude, this place is a madhouse," Theo whispered to Noah.

"Huh?"

"I said this place is a madhouse." A little bit louder this time.

"Ya think?"

"It's a lot more chaotic than the last time we came here. I can't tell if the jukebox is playing anything. I can't even hear myself think."

Suddenly, a glass broke, attracting everyone's attention.

"Whoops! Sorry everyone!" a drunk man yelled with a chuckle.

The bartender served the boys their drinks. "Here you go, guys."

Noah thanked the man and turned to Theo. "So what are we gonna do?"

"Just wait for later tonight, when you go to sleep. All we can do is hope, really."

A mysterious man wearing a brown leather jacket, dark blue jeans and a cap overheard them at the counter and looked up at them. He began to walk over. The boys noticed.

"So you guys haven't heard?" the man asked, his voice deep and gravelly.

"Heard what?" the boys replied.

"There's a solution," he remarked. He took his hat off and put it on the counter. "There are these people helping us. They're like, monks, or something. Oh yeah! Shamans. And they guide us through this mindfulness hour. Everyone sits silently and follows their orders."

"So it's just meditation?" Noah responded.

"Not exactly. It's some sort of ritual. So far, it hasn't been very successful, but that's only because they started a couple days ago. Everyone's confident it'll work, because they don't get those dreams."

"Wait, what? Seriously?" Theo asked.

"Yes, seriously. The best part is, their sessions are free. Basically what happened is those guys found out about what's going on, and since they weren't victims, they decided to try to help out everyone else dealing with it."

"And why aren't they victims?" Noah asked.

"Not sure," he replied. "I think it has something to do with meditating every day. They really are the wisest and strongest in the mind. Once you meet them, you won't be surprised."

"Take us there. We need this."

The man scratched his shaved beard and looked up, skeptical whether he should reveal the address of which the shamans preached their wisdom. Then, he took out a small piece of scrap paper he hid in his leather jacket, along with a short, worn-out pencil with little eraser left and most of the yellow bitten off from constant chewing. He wrote down the address and handed it to Noah.

"Remember," the man said. "Do as they tell you. They got a *lot* of people desperate for these sessions, so… Just don't be surprised if they have little patience."

Noah and Theo gave a confirming nod.

Later, the boys prepared to leave the bar.

Before they could walk out the door, the bartender exclaimed, "Hey! Aren't you guys gonna pay first?"

"Oh yeah! The drinks." Noah took $20 from his pocket and gave it to the bartender. "Keep the change."

With that, they departed.

The boys sat in the car. A shiny navy sedan. Surprising how they could keep it in such great condition after several years.

"So… a proper way to fix all of this? Is this it?"

"Let's not get ahead of ourselves. We've yet to meet these said shamans, and for all we know, that mysterious guy at the bar could've been setting us up for some sort of crime. Scammers do use things people desire to draw interest from their victims, you know."

"True, true… I'd still give it a chance, though. Whether it sounds legit or suspicious, we don't have much else to go off of."

Noah spoke whilst starting the car, "We'll just be extra careful then."

As they drove along the highway, Theo gazed through the window while making a man with his fingers, running atop the metal guardrails. The moonlight shone over the wide river by the city, making it glimmer like the stars above. The city lights glistened, and the skyline was dark. The roads were bustling with cars flashing headlights, just trying to make it home… or wherever they needed to go at 11 p.m. on a Friday night. The city was full of life. Theo saw it, and he noticed the plain land they were driving into. Boring. Blank. Full of nothing but potential. For now, its single use was for roads, apart from a few distant windmills.

After a brief hour of driving, they entered a town filled with little houses that looked like they couldn't fit more than a family of two. Not a single light was turned on; everyone seemed to be asleep or away from home. The sidewalks were lined with lush grass and clean yellow daffodils. The lawns of each house seemed to be well cared for, with most residents having sprinklers, perfectly mowed grass, pretty decorations and fancy shrubbery. The foliage around town was neat—not a single plant overgrowing or a leaf out of place. Trimmed trees, fallen leaves blown away, and overall a welcoming impression to any passing citizens.

Though it was hard to read each number in the pitch dark, Noah finally found the address of the said shamans' domain. The one house with lights turned on, dimly lit, and a long line of cars pulled up to the driveway. This lawn was nowhere near as neat as the others. Lots of tall grass, messy bushes, and leaves just lying on the ground. However, the residents seemed to have quite some attention.

This must be the place.

"Sit down, everybody; sit down; we haven't any time to waste!" a voice echoed, soft yet firm.

Everyone sat in a semicircle on a large wool rug in front of three people, who looked like they were in their thirties or sixties. To the side, shoes sat by the wall so as not to ruin the expensive carpet. In the middle sat one woman and two men.

They must have been the shamans. With their eyes closed, they patiently waited for everyone to settle down so they could begin the session. They wore full body cloths in black, covering everything but their heads. They looked similar to Buddhist monks (though their heads weren't shaved and both their shoulders were covered).

As soon as Noah and Theo arrived inside and saw what was going on, they immediately joined in by taking their shoes off and finding empty spaces to sit on the rug. They looked around to notice everyone sitting crossed-legged and upright, so they mimicked.

Soon, everything went silent. People waited patiently for the shamans to start their ritual and respected their desire for a quiet room to concentrate in. Even in a church or a library, you wouldn't be able to hear yourself blink.

"Join hands..." spoke the shaman sitting in the midst of his siblings.

Everyone obeyed. When Noah held hands with the people next to him, he felt a small sting, a static shock from socks on the carpet.

"Close your eyes," the woman continued.

The third spoke, "And imagine a haven. A place filled with nothing but tranquility and beauty."

Silence. After a while, Theo yawned.

"Now," the middle man spoke again. "Imagine yourself in the dream prison."

Some began to whimper. It was hard to keep the same silence now.

After a few minutes, the woman spoke, "Imagine yourself in the prison... with *power*."

"Imagine that you're not a convict. Imagine being lucid."

Silence.

"Everyone, open your eyes again, and relax. Let's help each other recognize this place more."

At the end of the semicircle, he gestured to someone to start sharing.

The plan here was to build such a detailed image of the prison that when you return there, your brain would recognize the place as a dream and become lucid. Would it work? Who knows. This was still an experiment anyway. Clearly, these three weren't the best at being therapists.

Everyone shared their experiences and observations, one after another. Some had tears in their eyes. Some fearless.

Soon after, the woman asked, "Does everyone know how to do a reality check? Raise your hand if you don't."

Noah and Theo raised their hands. No one else did.

The middle man addressed the boys, "Look at your hand. Make a fist. Then, one by one, lift all your fingers up. If you're in reality, you should see your five fingers clearly. In a dream, you might see more or less fingers, and it'll be less clear. Blurry, perhaps. When you remember to do a reality check in a dream and you realize you're dreaming, you just granted yourself lucidity."

The boys tried it. Five fingers, clear image, real life. Simple enough.

"Good. May we continue?"

They nodded. Everyone else sat there, staring at them, but the shamans' call broke their focus and redirected their attention. They commanded the group to meditate. This required no instruction.

An hour has passed. The room had been quiet and concentrated almost the entire time.

"Wake up."

Everyone finished meditating. Theo rubbed his eyes and yawned.

"Finally!"

Clearly bored by this setup, he was eager to finish. The whole time, he'd been napping. The crowd gave him a death stare. However, the shamans stayed calm, apparently used to occasionally boring people.

"Any updates?" the last shaman enquired.

"Well, I was kinda half asleep, half awake; I don't think I went to prison tonight." Theo's voice sounded rather refreshed despite his hour-long half-sleep.

The understanding shaman replied with a nod.

"Hold on," Noah blurted. "When I went to the dream prison, I was lucid. I knew I was dreaming. How come I couldn't wake up or do what I wanted?"

Without hesitation, the same shaman replied, "We know that. Everyone's '*lucid*'. Our job is to help you eradicate your fear of the five that hold you there and take back control of your mind. We do this by guiding our students through meditation and other activities."

"Like what?"

"Well, I'm glad you asked. We were about to begin."

Their stoic demeanors had perfectly hid their doubt in the process.

"Now," the middle man announced. "Who would like to demonstrate courage? Anyone, just come right up, look me in the eyes, and tell me that you're not afraid."

For a moment, no one dared stand up. Theo looked at Noah. Noah shrugged and gestured back, sending Theo to the shaman. He walked up confidently. He maintained eye contact with a serious face. The shaman sat unfazed. His face was expressionless, but his locked eye contact reflected intimidation.

"I…" Theo began, "I'm not afraid of you…" His voice was shaky.

He lost his false, emotionless expression. He proved his fear.

"Good try."

Theo sat back down next to Noah, absolutely humiliated, and it showed.

"Anyone else?"

No takers.

"Come on. This isn't good. Those Dreamers? They feed off your fear. The less willing you are to stand up and prove your confidence, the less freedom you'll have in there. Show us that you can handle breaking the chains of terror they put on you."

But alas, nobody had the courage to do it. Each person looked like they were waiting for someone to go before them, although they knew they couldn't. At this rate, no one would prove worthy of escaping the prison. The shamans whispered to each other. Their disappointment and concern were crystal.

"Well, maybe next time. Let's try a different approach. Who here has heard of mantras?"

No one raised their hand.

"A mantra," the woman spoke. "Is a word or phrase that you repeat over and over again, like when you try to remember something. It's a good way of getting a message across to your brain."

After the shamans elaborated, the circle recited their mantras non-stop. They were something like '*I'm not afraid*',

'It's just a dream', or *'Do a reality check'*. This creative change in plan felt like a milestone, with repeating voices echoing around the room, audibly more confident than the attendees seemed earlier.

When the session ended, everyone put their shoes back on, and Noah gave the shamans a polite handshake. Cars pulled out of the driveway; others walked home. Noah and Theo entered their sedan and drove away, leaving the strange village behind. It was now past midnight; not only were the boys sleepy but feeling disappointed as well. Those sessions… they couldn't help anything. They keep people there who continue to tell themselves that they're not afraid. But they *are* afraid. Who wouldn't be?

"That was total bullshit," Theo remarked. "I almost fell asleep to those bastards talking five times. How were those sessions supposed to help us?"

Noah, too tired to respond, shrugged and focused on the dim road ahead. Even if the sessions weren't genuinely helpful, he felt sincerity from the shamans, and he knew the attendees felt somewhat comforted by them.

Chapter 5

The crack of a massive whip shook Noah as he realized he was back in his prison cell. In the distance, a convict was being punished for who knows what, receiving continuous lashes from Magnus—with his mask off. Now, everyone could see his strawberry-blond hair and absolutely monstrous face. The screams were loud and terrible, giving everyone who witnessed it chills. Even if you couldn't see it, the immense, agonizing horror could be heard from afar.

Noah looked down at his hands.

Just do a reality check, he thought.

He put up his fingers, one by one on each hand, and when he held up ten, it was hard to count. Too blurry. Fingers shifting. More than ten, less than ten.

"That'll teach you, you disobedient scumbag!" Magnus' shout thundered after the final lash. "Who's next?" he screamed, scanning the area for a single soul who would let out a little sound.

Petrified, no one even dared whimper. After a terrifying five seconds of pure silence, Magnus' body vaporized on the spot, instantly teleporting to who knows where.

Noah sat down against the wall, his legs up, and his face covered by his arms. With all his might, he tried again.

Wake up… Wake up… You can do this…
That's what I like to see. Cry, cry…

"Huh?" Noah sprung up and completely shook. He looked around, hoping to see someone standing in front of his cell. No one there. Now completely paranoid, he sat with his eyes wide open, gazing through the cell bars.

Is he inside my head?
Why, yes, he is. Got something to hide?
Wait… what? Deepcity?
Huh?

Magnus popped out of thin air, standing in front of Noah's cell. He was furious.

"*How?*"

"Uh… I don't know… I don't know, I swear I did nothing!"

"*What do you think you're doing!*"

"I- uh- I…" Noah tried to speak. Nothing came out.
"You. Are. *So done!*"
In a dizzy, blurry minute, Noah saw nothing but black. Everything was quiet.

Wait… I woke up… Yes!

Noah opened his eyes, expecting to be lying in bed, to see his closet, to feel his pillow. He thought he'd taken one step closer to ultimate freedom. Instead, the sight of a new, more secure cell greeted him. The walls were smooth, dark gray metal, which felt like steel. Allegedly, it was stronger than any material in the real world. Instead of comprising bars, the door was solid, thick, and constructed from the same mysterious metal. There was a groove, separating the door in two: the bottom half, a trapezoid shape, and the top half, filling the rest. A rectangle of glass sat in the middle of the door, right above the groove. It was the smallest window Noah had ever seen. He tried to punch it, but alas, it didn't budge. Everything in this prison was unbreakable. Obviously. He inched closer to the door, peering outside his cell. It was an indoor block of higher-security prison cells, based on what he could see. Most of them were empty, apart from Noah and some other victims he could see. At the end of the hall, a Dreamer sat on a chair, watching each prisoner like a hawk. He wore all black, hood up, and his mask had the big white eye in the middle, like a lunatic's gaze. His black jacket had many pockets, and so did the black cargo pants. This Dreamer looked like a soldier who spent his life in an asylum, with a custom-made black army uniform, without the camouflage, and a special hood for extra anonymity.

The Dreamer, noticing Noah's appearance, stood up and walked over.

"What are you in here for?" the Dreamer asked.

Her voice revealed her gender. The mask made it impossible to tell otherwise.

Noah stared at her through the mini window of his cell, trying to think of a valid answer. If he were honest, he had almost no idea what was going on. What he did know was that he managed to see Magnus' dream, which angered him. But who would believe that?

"Hey! I'm waiting. Answer me!" the Dreamer exclaimed as she hit the door with her fist, now more annoyed.

"Uh... I don't know," replied Noah.

The Dreamer stepped back, put her hands behind her head, and looked away from him, as if she were taken aback with disbelief and frustration.

"Why must you make my job even more difficult? Just tell me the reason you're here! It's not that hard. You probably just acted disobedient or something!"

The Dreamer then advanced to the cell once again, leaning her arm on the door and lowering her head, so that the creepy mask covered the view through the glass.

"You're gonna tell me exactly what you did, so that I can validate it wasn't some mistake, and I can sit back on my chair and do my job. Understand? Now speak."

"Well," began Noah. "I had a dream. Before I found myself here. I saw this city, filled with business and anxiety. It was called *Deepcity,* a place that looked like the heart of an urban landscape. I suppose Magnus saw my memory of it because he was outraged when he got into my head. He knew that I saw his dream; it might've freaked him out, and now I'm here."

"You're lying... That's not possible."

Noah gave her a shrug and replied, "Well, believe what you want. It's not like I'm getting out of here anyway, so just leave me alone."

"If that's how it is, then I'll force my way into your thoughts!"

"Wait, wha—"

Before Noah could react, everything turned black. It was a whole minute until he found himself conscious again, but not in his bed nor in his cell. Instead, it was a smelly room, full of blank paintings. The first painting on the wall exhibited the detailed picture of *Deepcity,* and just like last time, they were tilted and turned. However, this time, there was one difference. The second canvas wasn't blank; it gradually filled up with lines, shapes, color, and finally, a label on the frame. *Undercity.* In this painting, the scene was just as busy as *Deepcity.* Vehicles drove everywhere on one of the countless layers of roads built, and people rushed to get to their destinations. The sky was substituted by a stone roof. This entire city landscape was underground. A hanging monorail system was attached to the mega ceiling. The train was clear in the front, leaving a blurry trail behind, highlighting its lightning speed. In the background, wide pillars held the ground up to prevent a collapse. They appeared to serve as conventional structures, embellished with lights and windows. Even with all this life, the atmosphere was dark and somehow eerie.

"Ugh, how can you live with hanging up a painting just to see it tilted like this? Does it really only bother me?" Theo complained, straightening each painting again, just like last time.

Then again, the hidden door made itself visible. Smoke and dust were released, filling the room. Then came the coughing, and sure enough, everything faded to black.

Finally, Noah had woken up in his own bed. Never had he felt so relieved. He opened his eyes, praying he wouldn't find himself in another sticky situation. But it was calm. Peaceful.

Refreshing. The light shafts squeezed between the curtains, brightening the room. The day was beautiful. The sun was casting warm, bright light everywhere. Birds were projecting their elegies happily, without a care in the world. Despite the joyful awakening in the pleasant morning, Noah's mind was still riddled with questions.

Am I in their heads? What the hell is going on? How will it all end?

No matter how much he tried to distract himself from the topic, his attention continued to draw back to the inevitable fate forced upon him.

Should I just accept what I can't change? Should I try to fight back? Should I give in and end the misery once and for all? No one will judge me... The intrusive thoughts creeped in like a parasite controlling his body. *No,* he thought. *I won't give them the satisfaction. I'll be here to the very end, even if it means—*

Just then, he heard a faint whisper in his head. It was he same voice that previously called to him.

You won't last... and I don't know what you're doing. But don't think it will work... Get out of my head, you psychotic bastard! Haven't you done enough? thought Noah.

What have I done? the voice answered.

You know damn well what you've done. Because of you, and your stupid little henchmen, countless people commit suicide every day. Mental health is a foreign term. Every night, just when you expect to fall asleep, relax, resting and forgetting about your troubles, your dreams also punish you. And for what? Why do you do this to us? Noah replied.

You deserve it. Each and every one of you.

What, and you don't?

Silence.

Well?

The voice faded away. The whispers were no more. The torment ended. At least for now.

Noah wished he had someone to talk to about all of this. Someone who could help. And besides the ridiculous hot water everyone was in, something in the back of Noah's head kept telling him that he was somehow special.

The others didn't dream of Deepcity, did they? So then, why me? What does it mean? Soon, he realized who he needed to go and see.

Noah arrived at the familiar town. He slowly drove around to find the right house. Sure enough, he recognized the house number and the messy yard of the shamans' house. He pulled up in their driveway, walked up to their door, and was about to knock when the door suddenly opened before him.

"Hello? What brings you here so early today?" asked one of the shamans.

"I'm here to discuss something really important. You probably get requests like these all the time, but I'm sure you've never been asked about this before, and I don't have anyone else like you to talk to."

The shaman stood there and thought for a moment. He looked skeptical. Then he replied, "Sure. Come on in then."

Noah walked over to the wool rug and began taking his shoes off when the shaman cut him off.

"You don't have to take your shoes off. Come sit over here." The shaman and gestured towards the kitchen, where a high counter and three high stools were located. Noah sat down.

The shaman offered refreshments.

"You like tea or coffee? Water perhaps?"

"Coffee, please. And where are the others?"

"They're meditating in another room. It's best not to disturb them. And how do you like your coffee?"

"Uh, I like any coffee. Usually, I just have an espresso, but make whatever you have."

The shaman nodded and grabbed a mug from an overhead cupboard.

"So... The reason I came here... I figured if anyone would understand, it would be you guys. It's just, something doesn't feel right. I know how bizarre this whole scenario is, with the world's population going to prison every night and stuff, heh, as if that were normal. But really, I have a story to tell."

"Go on then," spoke the shaman.

"The night before I came to the prison, I had a dream where I was in a stinky, white room full of blank paintings —"

The shaman stopped cold.

"What, you had it too?"

"Umm... Well, yes, in fact. I did. And did you happen to see one painting that wasn't blank? Something about a *Deepcity?*"

"Yes! That's exactly it. And my brother was there, straightening all the tilted canvases, and then a hidden door in the wall started to open. Dust and smoke blew out; we were coughing like crazy, and the dream ended."

"Weird. I was alone in that room, and there was no secret door. Speaking of which, where is your brother anyway? He didn't feel like coming?"

"Well, he didn't have share my concern. Besides, he wasn't too impressed with what he saw last session. But I know you guys have it; I know you're really trying. You just want to help."

"Yes," he replied, setting the mug on the counter for Noah. "Since we never experienced such a thing, it's hard to help people who describe such a phenomenon."

So it was true. Those three really were immune to the mind invasion.

"Anyway, back to the point. Magnus somehow read my mind and saw my memory of *Deepcity*. He sent me to a higher-security prison block. Barely anyone knew it existed, and hardly anyone was in there with me. Theo told me I attracted a lot of attention from the other prisoners after I disappeared. The Dreamer in the new block asked me what I did to end up there. I told her the truth, but she didn't listen. Then she tried to read my mind, and I blacked out. I returned to that little gallery, but another painting was filled in: *Undercity*."

The shaman hesitated. "You're special. It surprises me that they managed to trap you with the rest."

"I thought so too! But how? What makes me so different, and why me?"

"Before I say anything, there's something I should confess." The shaman sat down next to Noah with a tall glass of tap water. "About Magnus... He's not the mysterious, powerful overlord you think he is."

"Then who is he?"

"He is... our brother."

"*Huh?*"

"Let me explain. Us three and him are biological siblings. We grew up together. But Magnus... he's always been... different, to say the least. He was born mentally challenged. Nonetheless, we treated him as our fair and equal brother. We tried to make him feel loved and included. We four did everything together. We meditated, we learnt, and we played. Our relationship was strong. We felt inseparable. However, as we grew older, Magnus started to change. He was repulsive, pushed us away, and isolated himself when he shouldn't have. A sneaking suspicion grew in me that he would go his own dark way. I tried to ignore it, but the feeling only grew more. Soon enough, it turned out to be true. Magnus, at age eighteen, packed his things and left us in the dust."

"Well, what happened next?"

"We knew his dark side was taking over, and no one could really stop him. We predicted he would use his mental strength for evil."

"Couldn't you do *something?*"

"We absolutely could have. Perhaps we should have. But he was our brother. Despite his behavior and sudden changes in personality, we still loved him. It was too big a decision to do anything to him because of a little assumption, so we dropped it."

"And now we're here…"

"Back to the original subject, I think I figured it out."

"Wait, what about the other four Dreamers?"

"Just friends he picked up along the way. They must've learnt from him. Anyway, about the dreams. You said you blacked out when the second Dreamer tried to enter your mind. Then you had the dream. Do you know what this means?"

"Uhh…"

"Imagine you and Magnus on two sides of a valley. Magnus has a hook and tether, and he's about to throw it at you. The first time, you catch it. You remove the hook and throw the rope back to him. The second time, the hook caught you and pulled you into the valley."

"The valley being the prison."

"Exactly. I think the same logic applies. The next Dreamer came and tried to do the same, but you caught the hook."

"The hook being… what, dream essence?"

"That's my theory," the shaman said. He set down his glass and stared Noah dead in the eyes. "Your mind is strong—stronger than most. You have great potential. This isn't a matter of silly dreams. This is a power, and you need to learn to grow it. Control it. Use it against the Dreamers whenever you can."

"Okay… well, how do I do that?"

"Meditate every day. Try to get the Dreamers to break into your mind again so you can feel the connection. One day you will be able to mimic it. Build a bridge across that valley and confront the Dreamers head-on."

"Alright, you're making it sound so simple. Why don't you monks help out? You already meditate every day, you sound like you know what you're doing, and your minds are the strongest. If you don't get these prison dreams, you have the biggest advantage."

"We've been trying, but it seems impossible to force our way into the prison. We don't have that same connection. Besides, it's not something we *really* want to do."

Noah nodded and stared at the floor, contemplating said the words that had just come out. It was hard to hear, especially coming from this highly respected shaman, that he was so different. Special. Advantageous, even over the shamans.

"Alright then… I'll do it. I can meditate every day. I can attract the Dreamers' attention. I will grow this power. I'll do my best."

"We wish you the best of luck."

"I'm sorry, what did you say your name was again?"

The shaman hesitated, then replied, "Alexander. And the other two are Evie and Vivian."

With a nod, Noah responded, "See you around."

"I look forward to meeting you again soon."

Chapter 6

Theo walked in on Noah sitting on his bed, facing the wall. His legs were crossed, and his eyes were closed.

"What the hell are you doing?" Theo questioned.

No response.

"Did they brainwash you? Why are you meditating?" Once again, no response.

"...Why are you ignoring me?" Frustrated, he continued, "Well, I'm going to the grocery store. Do you want anything?" Theo did not expect an answer.

"Pizza bites," Noah responded.

Theo rolled his eyes, let out a heavy sigh, and left the room.

An hour later, Theo returned with the groceries. Noah wasn't meditating anymore; he was sitting on the couch, watching clips of insane moments in his favorite soccer matches.

"It's an absolute ghost town out there."

"Hm?"

"It doesn't seem real, seriously. Couldn't see a single person on the streets. Most places were actually closed. I found six people in the supermarket, and four of them were staff."

"I wonder why everyone's at home."

"Hmm, I wonder," Theo replied sarcastically and slightly aggressively.

"Oh wait, I did actually find one guy roaming around on the sidewalk. He seemed very depressed and burnt out. I guess everyone's traumatized."

"The apocalypse will come soon…"

"Okay, are you actually *excited* for an apocalypse or something? Why do you keep mentioning it?"

"It's the most realistic outcome. The brain is the most powerful part of you, and when it's messed with and your mental health is put to the ultimate test, people can do things you never expected to happen."

"I guess you're right, but do you really have to say that every time? I don't want to be reminded of a coming apocalypse every time I talk about it being quiet outside."

"More than quiet. And I'd enjoy it while it lasts."

"Noah!"

"Okay, okay, sorry. But you know it'll happen eventually."

"Let's hope for the best, eh?"

"Alright, man, but I'm telling you. Mark my words: the more time that passes, the closer people will get to their breaking points. Even us. Having no control over your mind is a lot to handle. Terrifying."

"Oh, but just go meet up with the shamans and meditate every day! That'll fix everything!"

"Ugh, you wouldn't understand. I'm trying to be real here." Noah sighed. "Sorry for constantly mentioning an apocalypse. Not that I'm hoping for one to happen, but you know…"

"Yeah… And what do you figure will happen in this said apocalypse?"

"Time will tell. My hypothesis—"

"My hypothesis," Theo mocked. "Sorry. Continue."

Noah gave Theo a piercing glare. "I predict a tsunami of suicides. No one will be able to take it. The economy will crash, and no one will be able to provide anything."

"So what, people just kill themselves and the country falls quiet?"

"Poor mental health also leads to crime. And oh boy, be prepared for a hell of a lot of that."

"Oh… right. Well, what now?"

"What now? Well, I'm actually kinda hungry. Did you get those pizza bites?"

"Only the last box," replied Theo with a hyped tone.

The boys warmed up the pizza bites and devoured them. Before they knew it, there were none left.

"They never last long enough," Noah remarked.

"So… about you meditating…"

"Yeah?" Noah answered before his head violently fell onto the table with a shriek.

He put his hands on his ears and shook his head repeatedly, murmuring something unclear to himself. It was Magnus.

Get out of my head! Fuck off!

Nice to speak with you too.

What the hell do you want with me?

Well, calm down. I can't do anything to you right now, can I?

Says the one forcing his way into people's minds to torture them into committing suicide! You're a monster, you know that?

And what are you gonna do about it?

Fuck you! You know none of us can do anything; that's why you continue!

Oh? Was it not you who also made his way into my mind?

I don't even know how I did that! Coincidence? Telepathy? I don't know; I'm just confused!

You're endangering us, Noah.

Wha- h- huh? How?

You tell me.

I told you already, I have no idea! This is stupid! Speaking of which, you never made it clear why you started this whole shebang.

You all deserve it; you must be punished!

What, and you don't? What makes every single human deserve this treatment?

"Noah?" Theo called. Noah finally heard.

Answer me!

Theo tapped Noah on the head. It looked as though Noah had just woken up from a forced slumber. He slowly rose back up and looked at Theo with a mixed expression of fear and rage. Theo was shocked and scared as he asked Noah what that was all about. He explained how Magnus could use telepathy outside of people's sleep states. Theo looked horrified and sickened at the thought that Magnus had people's minds in his grasp and that this crisis was more than a dream. And from this point on, it would only get worse.

Noah would go out to buy groceries. Over time, more people gradually filled up the city, making it look rather normal. But as time went on, Noah noticed a pattern. Many people walking around looked shady. Many were smoking, doing and dealing drugs, and in less open areas, murdering. The rise in crime was happening, just like he'd predicted. Shoplifters stole from shops and convenience stores, urging them to close. Craters, dirt and trash littered the streets and sidewalks. The city was a hell hole.

Eventually, an event happened that sparked the beginning of the *ultimate* apocalypse.

When people gave up being civilized. It was every man for himself, leaving no time for rest. Everyone guarded their possessions with their lives, even if they were as small as a handful of grapes.

Noah was walking home from his regular grocery trip, which was getting increasingly difficult to complete with the rapidly diminishing stock. The roar of cars' horns honking and beeping echoed far down the street, as a pale man stood atop the roof of his car, blocking all traffic. Noah peered at the distant road. The man had pink eyes with dark bags under them and messy hair, wearing clothes stained all over. Some of the marks were brown, like coffee. Others were more dirty. He looked as if he hadn't looked at a bed for weeks; let alone be bothered to maintain any hygiene.

"I've had just about enough of this bullshit!" the man exclaimed hoarsely, his voice shaky yet threatening. "Can't you all see? We're prisoners of this endless madness! No matter how hard we try, we can't escape this... *purgatory* that we've fallen into!"

The drivers' impatient noise slightly died down as some tried to listen. In the distance, you could still hear a couple of beeps and honks. The sound of the poor man's voice, however, dominated the road, stealing all attention from the traffic and nearby crowds.

"You probably realized it already, maybe not, but our lives have already ended!"

"Nothing matters anymore!"

With that, he quickly reached into his pocket and pulled out a remote device. No one thought to think twice about what it could've been. As the man brandished it and stomped his feet like a lunatic, screams flew around the city. He let out an evil, hysterical laugh and shriek, and soon, his thumb landed on the button.

Explosions demolished the buildings they'd been planted in and pierced the ears of everyone around. Citizens scattered, sprinted and scrambled, utterly horrified, like ants frantically dashing around to avoid falling pebbles. Debris continuously crashed down, crushing people and their vehicles and blocking every corner of the street. It was now that everyone knew for sure that the waking world had descended into chaos. Noah's eardrums almost burst from the noise of the explosion, and the shockwave knocked him back a little. It was horrifying to experience in real life. Noah was paralyzed for a minute before he realized he needed to get out of there immediately.

In the dream world, Dreamers built up fear and concern against Noah by the night. All the meditation seemed to work. The more the Dreamers saw their dreams in Noah's head, the less stable their minds became. The paranoia was unstoppable. Dreamers refused to breach Noah's mind because the consequences were too much to handle. The counterattacks seemed inevitable, and Noah was gaining too much power. One time, a Dreamer was so stressed about it, she accidentally let the convicts run free from solitary confinement. Magnus had never forgiven her for that. Only one other Dreamer was on Magnus' side against her, while the others understood that it wasn't her fault. Prisoners were baffled because of the persistent quarrels among all five Dreamers arguing all the time, and despite their anxieties, they experienced relief in their temporary neglect.

Noah also attracted lots of attention from fellow prisoners. They saw him as a legend for scaring the Dreamers so often. When anyone asked what Noah's secret was, he would never give a distinct answer. The shamans also received mentions of Noah and his outstanding acts and behavior in the prison. They also refused to answer similar questions.

As tensions rose in both worlds, with warmongers fighting in the waking world and wardens beefing in dreams, everyone questioned which realm was safer. Was the prison even worth avoiding at this point?

But one night, a seemingly ordinary time at the prison, there were no Dreamers in sight.

When one man slammed his fist against his cell bars, exclaiming "Hey Dreamers! Where are ya? Give up so soon?"

His door opened immediately. He curiously walked out, and a cloud of pure black smoke rushed down to him. It quickly came together to resemble a man. Soon enough, the smoke cleared, and his features were clear. He was at least six feet tall, bald, ragged clothes, dark skin, carrying a black balisong.

He stared the man dead in the eyes before he lunged, in a thick Nigerian accent saying, "Let me make an example of you."

Once his foot left the ground, his body turned into a cloud of smoke again. The smoke spun around the man like a cyclone, hindering his vision. Suddenly, the balisong appeared and spun around quicker than any professional could've done. In its open state, it aimed at the man and slashed his rib. The knife struck again, this time from the other side. Back and forth, the knife flew at the man exponentially faster, cutting hundreds of slits in his flesh. To finish, a big, final slash sliced his neck, sending his head flying a few meters away. Afterwards, the smoke collected itself again, with the man spinning his knife to its closed state and putting it in his pocket.

He looked down at the corpse's head and separated bits of flesh and said, "Rest in pieces, insolent one!"

With that, he spat on the corpse and flew off.

"Who the hell was that guy?" Theo asked the next morning.

"A sixth Dreamer? What was so special about him? Where are the others?"

"How do we know the others aren't still there? We only saw him last night."

"I guess."

"But I feel like something must've happened for them to get a new guy in. And I don't like this. He is *not* to be messed with."

"Yeah, no kidding."

"And whoever he is, he's more powerful than an ordinary Dreamer. At least, that's what it looked like. It would make sense if he was temporarily replacing the original five while they do something else. That way, they don't have to worry about hiring another five Dreamers when they can instead hire one new, even more powerful, Dreamer."

"But that begs the question: what could they be doing? It has to be something real world related, right? But what?"

"Could someone have found them? The FBI or CIA perhaps?"

"I don't know," Noah replied anxiously. "As much as we'd love to think that, something deep down just doesn't feel right. In fact, it feels very, very wrong…"

"What the fuck does that mean, Noah? They're *building* their empire or something?"

"Do we want to find out?"

"Well, how do you plan to stop them, monk?"

Noah shut his eyes tight, and his head fell down. Theo looked at him, confused, thinking maybe Magnus was attacking again. After about ten seconds, Theo was about to speak when he heard a faint whisper, not coming from any direction but in his head.

Theo…

"Ah! It's Magnus! Noah! Help!"

We... will... be...
"Get out of my damn head!"
Safe...

"What do you mean you'll be *safe*?"

Suddenly, the whispering stopped, but Theo still felt new knowledge flowing in. Like an instinct. An intuition. He suddenly knew it couldn't have been Magnus doing that.

"Wait... that wasn't Magnus... Was it?"

Noah lifted his head again and opened his eyes.

"No..." spoke Noah, slowly shaking his head at Theo with a subtle grin.

Theo's eyes widened, and his jaw dropped in great epiphany as he felt an immediate overload of jubilation.

It's time to balance... the power...

Chapter 7

Theo, relaxing on the couch, listening to his favorite music, felt his phone vibrate with a text notification. He opened it curiously to see an unknown number attempting to persuade him to come to *the alley behind John Doe's beef butchers at 10 p.m. tonight*. The messenger promised hundreds of dollars in exchange for all known information about the Dreamers.

"Hey Noah, check out this shady ass message I got just now."

"Um…" Noah was visibly concerned about this, and he seemed lost for words. "I don't know, man. You'd better lay low. Whoever sent you this knows our location, so you should stay inside and away from the windows."

"Look, I know it's suspicious, but what if the man just wants help?"

"Why the hell would he tell you to meet *there* at *that* time? And why would he ask *you*?"

The messenger sent another text. This time, it was a selfie of a seemingly troubled homeless man on the verge of tears. He had a messy gray moustache and beard, and was wearing a stained beige hoodie and a dirty black vest on top. *Please,* the messenger begged.

Theo replied, *"Why me? I don't even know you. It's awfully suspicious of you to text a random number to meet at a random location and offer hundreds of bucks."*

Once again, the mysterious man replied, *I'm doing this to everyone I can find. I know you live nearby because of a post you made online. I'm looking for people in the area who can tell me anything about the Dreamers. Together, we can stop them.*

Noah glared at Theo.

"Don't do it, man; he's asking for trouble."

"I know I should be cautious and all, but desperate times call for desperate measures. I can't be all that surprised that someone resorted to doing this in search of information."

"I don't care. It's unsafe. You're being naïve again, and right now, we can't have that."

"But... I want to help..."

"So do I! But when you see a shady text message like this, you can't *possibly* think this is a safe option! Remember all the crime? The apocalypse, y'know? Trust me, you need to decline his offer. Plus, look at him. Does he look like the kind of man who has hundreds of dollars in pocket money?"

Theo looked at the selfie again.

"Maybe he stole it?"

"Doesn't matter! This is for our own safety. I can't believe you're considering doing this."

Theo frowned and nodded.

I know I look shady. I wouldn't believe me either if I were you. But with a little information, I can do amazing things. I can show you if you want, but you'll have to be here. I just need to put an end to this whole shebang, yk?

That's it, Theo thought.

He was going over there, whether Noah approved or not.

10 p.m.

"Hello? Anyone there?" Theo called at the meeting place.

"Theo? Where are you?" Noah called. No answer. Theo had left. "Theo!" Still no reply. "I know you can hear me! Remember to do the dishes!"

But alas, Theo was away. It was only a matter of time before Noah realized he'd gone to the meeting place with the shady man. His inner child has taken over once again, just like it always has.

Noah searched the house, checking each room and knocking on closed doors. Theo was nowhere to be found. Noah called him, but there was no answer. Then he pulled out his phone to dial Theo. He heard no ring, which meant Theo had his phone with him. Then it hit.

You're done for… Any last words? said Magnus in Noah's head once again.

Shut! Up! I'm sick of your drama! I'm sick of you, your henchmen, and your stupid fucking prison you set up for a reason you still refuse to share! Just leave! Get out of my head!

I-leave!

Then the voice stopped. This now felt like routine to Noah. But more importantly, he had to liberate Theo from the mess he got himself into. He jumped in his car, quickly recalled the spot, and zoomed off with the greatest urgency.

When he arrived, there was no sign of his brother or the man who called him there. Nothing to be seen. He looked around for any traces, but alas, they were long gone. Noah persisted in his search for about half an hour before deciding to return home, completely defeated. When he got back, he quickly called the police and told them what happened. Noah didn't expect much help from the police at a time like this, and frankly, he was correct.

"We can't open a missing person case before thirty-six hours have passed," they told him. "Go check morgues, hospitals, wherever, and use traditional methods first. Then, we'll consider taking action."

Noah planned on wasting no time on this hunt.

He hopped back into his car and raced around the city looking for any signs of his brother. After a couple of exhausting hours of searching, he remembered the advice the officers gave him. *Hospitals and morgues.* Noah sped to the nearest hospital, maintaining his speed just barely under the limit. When he arrived, he zoomed to the front desk to ask about any new patient admissions.

"I need to find my brother," began Noah frantically. "Did anyone new come to this hospital in the last twelve hours or so? His name is Theo; he—"

"Now hold on," the lady at the front desk interrupted. "Slow down. Let me pull up the records."

After thirty seconds of waiting, Noah impatiently asked, "Are you done?"

"Hold on, I have to log in first," she responded.

Log in? The hell?

"We don't have time for this…" Noah muttered under his breath.

"Okay, so what were you saying again?"

"I'm looking for my brother. He's twenty-eight, blond hair, uh, brown eyes…"

"Could you be any more specific, please?" Her voice could not possibly sound more uninterested. Noah was visibly agitated by this.

"Yeah, he's about five feet eight inches tall, Caucasian, not very muscular…"

"Sir, we actually didn't have any new patient admissions in the last twelve hours. The crime must be slowing down out there."

Why did she wait until now to tell me that?

"Uh… any new persons in the…" Noah's heart ached to finish the sentence. His voice trembled as he continued, "…Morgue?"

"One second," the disinterested nurse replied as she slowly navigated her way through the computer system. She typed as slowly as an elderly person using their first desktop.

Damn! Hurry up!

"We got one person in last night that kinda matches your description… John Doe, pronounced dead upon arrival… We haven't identified him yet."

Noah's heart ached even more. He felt a drop of sweat roll down his forehead as he fervently hoped this wasn't his dead brother.

"So... would you like someone to escort you to the morgue?"

In the same fearful voice, Noah reluctantly replied, "Yes..."

"Alright then. Please tell me your name and sit in the waiting area over here while we find an escort to help you out. You will need to fill out a verification form before visiting; have proof of relationship and identifications at the ready."

"Noah Bennett... Thank you," he quickly responded and walked to an empty seat.

The wait was the longest five minutes of Noah's life. Each second felt like a minute, and each minute felt like an hour. His impatience was unbelievable—he was biting his nails, tapping his foot, his red face covered in sweat—someone across the room asked him to quiet down.

Eventually, a coroner walked down the hall and called out, "Noah Bennett?"

Noah's heart raced as he stood up and walked to the coroner.

"Follow me," he said. He took Noah to an empty room with a desk and a couple of chairs. In front of one of the chairs on the desk was a form.

"You will need to fill out this form before we can allow you to proceed."

Noah sat down in front of the paper and began answering the questions. Some required identification. Luckily, Noah responsibly kept such on his phone. When he finished, he handed the form to the coroner. He inspected the answers carefully, and at the end, he handed the form to a nearby assistant.

"Come with me," the coroner told Noah.

His heart raced even faster.

Walking into the room of the morgue was haunting. Tonnes of drawers in the walls, full of corpses. Drawers were marked with numbers, and most of them had accompanying names. It almost felt sinister to Noah, with all these bodies that used to be people, collected here like disposable objects.

The coroner led Noah to the correct drawer, which he opened.

"Well?" the coroner asked.

Hesitantly, Noah pulled the cover. He almost couldn't bear to look; his instinct told him what he was about to see. He tried to escape the thought, but the gut feeling was too strong. As he slowly pulled the cover all the way down, he opened his eyes and saw the perfect resemblance of Theo's body. A wide bullet hole right in the center of his forehead majorly deformed his face, causing it to bleed. The pain Noah felt was unbearable. The sight was horrifying, and his emotional reaction was visceral. He teared up immediately as he sobbed, clinging to his dead brother's body, disregarding anything else.

With a nod, the assistant silently asked the coroner if this was a positive identification.

The coroner nodded back, silently mouthing a, "Yeah."

Noah's crying lasted over ten minutes before he stood up and whispered to the body, "Goodbye, Theo…"

Tears still ran down his cheeks, but it was time to move on. The coroner pulled the cover back up and closed the drawer as he escorted Noah out of the room.

After a devastating trip to the morgue, where the horrible news broke and Noah fell into great despair, it was time to report the truth to the police. With all the grief and sadness built up, Noah could hardly bring himself to start the car. Before he could take off to the station, he just sat in the driver's seat, head on the wheel, and cried his heart out.

The original Dreamers were back at the prison, but the Black Butterfly, as people called him, was nowhere to be seen. When Magnus saw Noah sitting in his usual cell, he had to look twice before flying to him in complete shock.

"What is it this time?" Noah asked in pure resentment.

Magnus was almost speechless until he uttered, "But how? You died!"

"No fuckwit, you killed my brother! Are you proud of yourself? Why would you even do that? Why *him?*"

"I never killed your brother…"

"The fuck you mean you never did? I'm still grieving over his death after the police showed me what happened! Now you wanna play stupid?"

"No… I sent a man to kill *you.* I don't care about your brother…"

Noah's heart sank. This response had him totally lost for words. He was trying to open his mouth, but nothing came out. He felt like he had just escaped death.

"They must've got the wrong—"

"Is that supposed to help me?" interrupted Noah, overpowered by rage. *"As if this torture weren't far enough! Now you try to kill us in the real world?"*

"I—"

"Don't even start on that 'death is a mercy' shit! When I get out of here, I am going to—"

Before Noah could finish his rant, Magnus disappeared in an instant. Noah let out a loud grunt as he slammed his fist into the cell door.

I will make him pay! he thought to himself.

The following morning, Noah finally arrived at the station. Sitting at the front desk was another man, but Noah didn't care. He rushed to him with the news.

"Hey! I found my brother. He was in the morgue. Shot in the face, and I know who did it. I have the murderer's confession."

"Excuse me?"

"Yesterday someone told me to check the hospitals and morgues and whatever for my missing brother, so I did."

"And now you want to report a murder, do you?"

"Yes."

"Alright then, you'll have to tell me any information you know about the murderer and proof of confession."

"Well… I don't have proof of confession, but his name is Magnus—"

"Wait, *the* Magnus?"

"Uh, yeah. He told me—"

"Hold on, this changes everything. If we can trace the murder to him, we can catch him for good and end the entire dream scheme!"

"Great!"

After the successful hunt for Theo and the trip to the police station, Noah was feeling quite proud of himself as he tried to relax on the couch. Noah had effectively fulfilled his role in pursuing vengeance. The police had the job of doing everything they could to catch Magnus, or at least, the man he sent. Although there was nothing for Noah to help with, he still felt guilty and almost lazy for waiting. Even after today, the grief of Theo's death was deeply rooted in him, making a true rest nearly impossible to achieve because of the perpetual whirling of thoughts, memories, and emotions. After sharing the home with Theo since he was eighteen, living alone felt like a new, foreign routine. Every meal, every TV program, every story—none of it was ever the same. Every time Noah saw medication on a counter, it reminded him of Theo. During the night, when Noah was going to sleep, his room held no trace of his brother, and as he lay in bed, there was triggered in him a ruthless tornado of feelings that were too extreme for anyone to bear. *Justice will be served,* he thought.

"*You didn't die in vain*," he told himself.

Theo's death was, by far, the biggest factor fueling Noah's motivation to bring down the Dreamers for good.

8 a.m.

The doorbell rang. Luckily, Noah was already awake—just barely—gulping coffee and contemplating things. He went to the door curious as to who could be visiting his house at this hour, and was greeted with an unexpected sight.

"Huh?"

"Hello, Noah."

Chapter 8

Two agents stood there. They wore black suits, black-tinted glasses and earpieces. The man stepped forward and pulled out his wallet with his badge and identification.

"Agent William Anderson, Federal Bureau of Investigation. Pleasure to meet you. Do you mind if we come inside and have a little talk?"

Noah hesitated.

"Oh, yeah, no, come in. Can I get you guys anything?"

"Don't bother. We want to talk to you about your new nemesis, Magnus."

"Oh—"

"Tell me, Noah, even after everything he's done, why did he go out of his way to target *you?* We've heard it was the first incident of him getting involved in real life."

"Well… this may be hard to believe, but… I'm kinda inside his head."

The agents leaned forward, intrigued by this response.

"Tell us more," the female agent said.

"Yeah. Well, it all started before I started having those dreams in prison. I had a dream where I was in a white room full of paintings, all of which were blank except one. Apparently, that painting represented one of Magnus' dreams.

He found out about it, scolded me for it, and sent me to the higher security block. I was confused, but I had guidance."

"Is that all?"

"Who did you have guidance from?"

"Well, these neighborhood shamans… monks… whatever you might call them, gave me some advice. My mental state has strengthened since then, and I now have the 'dream powers'. I guess it was too much for them to handle, so Magnus hired a hitman to kill me. He admitted to me that the hitman made a mistake and killed my brother instead. I miss him so much…"

The agents looked at each other in awe and took out notepads.

"This is a lot. Can you repeat some of that for us?"

Noah explained the story again, answering all their questions. They filled their books with every last detail. After confirming that they had recorded everything important, they stood up and began to leave.

They opened the door, but before they exited, the man turned back and said with a smirk, "By the way, we're not done with you. We got your back."

"What does that me—"

The agents had left. Noah was on his own. Or was he? What did they mean by that? Were they coming back to protect his home? To bring personal bodyguards? Either way, it would be nice to have some extra protection after being targeted by Magnus in the real world.

The next day, Noah opened the door to two different agents. Their uniforms were navy, labelled with bold yellow letters: 'FBI'. They wore vests; they had epaulettes on their shoulders, and the belts on their waists held utilities such as flashlights and pistols.

"Uh, hello? Can I help you?"

One man replied, "We were sent to bring you to a safer place."

"A safer place? Do I want to come?"

"If you want to survive with the knowledge that you're under heavy protection, yes."

"And... what if I decline?"

The man stepped forward, now eye-to-eye with Noah.

He took off his glasses and continued, "Noah, listen to me. Arguably, the most powerful man in the world is harassing you. If you sit here in your own house, completely open to being attacked, doing nothing to defend yourself, he will come for you again and *ensure* that the job is done. Is that what you want?"

"I guess not... but where will you take me?"

Gorwood Penitentiary

The halls were filled with the piercing noise of screams, bangs, crashes and chatter among the prisoners.

"I cannot believe you brought me to a prison..."

"Don't worry, this is the safest place we know of. Three men watch you at all times, under maximum security. Only one of *our* wardens can tell them to rest or stop their shifts. This will only happen if another man is available to take over. You'll be safe from the prisoners and outside dangers. By the way, we will provide food for you free of charge. And none of that nasty prison food shit the others get to eat. Proper meals."

"Well, I guess that's nice."

They made their way to Noah's new cell. The room was prepared for his arrival, and he had to admit it looked rather nice. However, despite being nicer than the other cells, it was still visibly one of them. The windowless brick walls and the bed next to the bathroom didn't give a very comforting vibe, nor did the screams and shouts of the prisoners in the cafeteria.

Noah sat down on the bed. He looked around, observing his new cell. It wasn't something that would be easy to get used to.

"Now remember, if you need anything, just ask us, Alright?" one of the officers asked.

He gave Noah a thumbs-up, nodded, and walked away.

There was no internet, no TV, and nothing to do except meditate. So that's what Noah did. He meditated for hours until it was lights out. The noisy and uncomfortable environment made meditation a real challenge. However, with the correct state of mind, it didn't get in his way.

Shortly after Noah found comfort under the covers, he found himself awoken in prison once again. Dreamers flew around like phantoms in search of their next victims. Back and forth, like a tennis match between two sides of the place. Sometimes, Noah had noticed that the Dreamers would give him a weird look of fear and disturbance. When Magnus came by, the look would be more like a death stare of fury. Each glare from a Dreamer filled Noah with dopamine, reminding him of his power and status in the situation despite being a victim of the vicious predators that placed him there.

"Hey, Noah! Can I ask you something?" said a man in a neighboring cell.

The question caught the attention of a Dreamer levitating nearby.

"Hm? What is it?"

"Hey! I wouldn't talk to this man. Do you have any idea what he's done?"

Oh man, I really don't feel like being here tonight…

While the Dreamer scolded and lectured the man with indoctrinating garbage, Noah stared at him. Then something slowly started to click. The Dreamer quickly peered back at Noah with a "Huh?"

"Hey! Who's the guy in that cell you're guarding?"

"Come on, tell us! This isn't fair!"

"It's none of your concern," replied an agent.

"What makes *him* so special to you guys?" another convict cried.

"Yeah! Isn't he one of us? Let us through!"

The prisoners screamed the phrase in unison, "Let us through! Let us through!"

Noah could hear the sounds of chanting, fighting, and brutal beatings. He ran to the cell window. Because of their curiosity, a full-on riot had started. Noah tried his best to ignore them, for his own sake. Besides, he had other things to focus on, and this prison made him feel closer to Magnus than ever. He wondered if this was the exact prison Magnus was sent to before he started his own.

Later, when the prisoners were in their cells and the chaos died down, Noah felt like stretching his legs. He was allowed to roam around, as long as he was accompanied by his bodyguards. After half an hour of sitting in the yard enjoying the sunlight, he had to use the bathroom. He asked if there were any nearby, besides the toilet in his cell. His agents escorted him there.

With his only source of protection waiting outside, Noah walked to a urinal. Before he could unzip his pants, he heard a stall door open behind him. A convict walked out.

"You're the person!" he shouted.

"Hey, shouldn't you be in—"

He cut Noah off mid-sentence by bashing him in the head with a rock. Before Noah passed out cold, he could faintly hear his bodyguards rushing in and dealing with the attacker, but it was too late.

The next thing he saw was the blurry vision of a cuboid. It was blue, yellow, or gray; he wasn't really sure. The sky was still blue and filled with puffy clouds. It was impossible to recognize anything else. Soon enough, Noah woke up from this strange dream in a haze.

The Infirmary – Day 1

The monitor beeped, the agents discussed, and the nurses frantically struggled to help Noah.

"Look, his eyes are open!"

Almost completely oblivious to his surroundings, all Noah realized was the bandages on his head, the throbbing of the wound, and the unfamiliar bed he was lying on.

"You gave him the correct dosage, right?"

"Of course!"

Noah, half-awake now, sat up in his bed.

"What happened?"

An agent knelt down beside him.

"What happened was you suffered a concussion. We can wait twenty minutes for you to feel better, and then we'll have to do some tests."

"What tests?"

"Memory. Emotions. Nerves. Stuff like that."

After a while, Noah, still dizzy, decided he felt ready to take the test. Until he mentioned Theo, everything he gave seemed to add up right. Something that would've wiped any smile off his face now seemed to do the opposite. He smiled. He silently giggled. Soon, he started laughing. The agents looked at each other then wrote on their clipboards.

Why am I laughing? It's not funny... Theo was a good guy...

Besides that, Noah's responses and actions were mostly normal, and his mindset was mostly unchanged.

Later, Noah realized he still hadn't used the toilet. He really needed to go now. He asked the agents, and since the infirmary had no risk of rogue prisoners running around, they allowed him to go. One bodyguard followed him. After he got back, he asked the nurses what they dosed him with. He remembered overhearing something about being given medicine. They told Noah that they injected him with morphine, which they were confident would have no severe side effects. He didn't notice any side effects either, so everything must've been fine.

The Infirmary — Day 2

After last night in the infirmary, Noah realized something. The time of his stay in dream prison had reduced. Also, he had another odd dream about an outdoor box. However, this time, it was more vivid. It felt real. And it wasn't just a box. It was a house. The windows were much clearer, with the inside lighting shining out and the grass around more distinctly green and lush. The vision outside the house was short though—it was followed by a view from the inside. All Noah saw was a dining room table with three lights above, hanging from the ceiling.

That morphine did have a side effect, didn't it? My dreams... They're less cluttered by the prison, more free... and lucid. Well, the prison was lucid, but when I wasn't in prison, I still felt so. And what could this apartment be? Where is it, and what does it mean? I've always known dreams can be... rather pointless, random and confusing, but I've always believed that each one had a deeper meaning. This isn't an ordinary house.

Before the agents and nurses could wish Noah a good morning, he let out a burst of information. He claimed to have seen an apartment in his dream, and it was a dream like he'd never had before.

"What's that supposed to mean?" asked one of his bodyguards.

"I think they could be there. Y'know, the Dreamers."

"Look, we know you're a different case, but isn't this a little—"

"Wait," another agent replied, interrupting him. "He could be onto something. We've always seen potential in him. Remember the reason we're doing this in the first place? He's not some random guy we decided to protect. He has the same sorta telepathic magic they have. At least hear him out; it might match with one of our leads."

The agents looked at Noah.

"Tell us what you saw, Noah."

One was hesitant to comply.

"Thank you. Well, what I saw wasn't much, but I did see the sky, some grass, a house with big windows, and a dining table with three hanging lights above it."

"Do you have any ideas where it could be?"

"Well, probably near a park? If I did see grass. I'm not sure. The inside looked kinda small, so maybe an apartment building. Those apartments in the city also have big windows, so maybe it could be somewhere there. But it seems like an odd place for the Dreamers to hide."

The agents wrote down everything on their notepads.

"Do you think this was their plan? To hide in plain sight, because they expected us to search further out?"

"I… don't know."

"Well, let me make something clear. We can't waste time with these dreams, especially when they're not even reliable. I'm not saying you would lie to us, but it's our work to use what we have and work *quickly*. If you have any more of these visions, tell us, but in the meantime, we gotta keep looking."

"So…"

"What I'm saying is, we can't wait for you to have visions, but we can use the info you gave us. I can almost guarantee you that we'll put your word to good use."

"That's good to hear," replied Noah, nodding.

Later that day, Noah's agents updated him on the search. They looked into areas with parks nearby and kept track of specific buildings that had abnormal behaviors. One of the apartments' residents only used the back door. Another apartment always had its lights off, even at night, but had regular pizza deliveries every week. The agents thanked Noah for the lead and assured him that everything was going smoothly.

The hospital food Noah had to eat for lunch was unappetizing. He was served a plate with peas, rice and chicken—all the quality you would expect from food on an airplane. However, they did allow him to order food from restaurants, fast food or vendors. They treated Noah to a nice medium-rare steak with mashed potatoes and carrots for dinner, which was much better than what the infirmary provided.

Every four hours, Noah had to take a tablet of morphine to ease his head pain. While the pain did go away, he was still concerned about the side effects it could've had. It messed with his brain, which was what he needed most right now.

Before Noah went to bed, he saw Theo standing beside him. He knew it wasn't real. He laughed.

"What are you doing here?"

"Your mind… It's messed up."

"Yeah, you don't say."

"I still believe you can do this."

Noah laughed again.

"Your concussion makes my tragedy funny."

"Theo…"

Theo walked closer to Noah, then continued.

"You'll get better soon. You'll beat them. You'll win."

"But what if I can't?"

"Tell me again, why do you still try?"

"You got this. Don't give up."

Theo's body faded away, but his words were glued inside Noah's head. It was all he could think about as he went to sleep.

Noah found himself in the dream prison again. He proceeded to wear the hospital gown, and the bandages were still wrapped around his head. Since he started losing contact with the Dreamers, they paid less attention to him, although he was still haunting them in the back of their minds. This sentence flew by quickly, as he found himself next inside the same house. Although he was paralyzed in one spot, more details were unveiled: a wooden staircase, a large carpet, a high ceiling…

The Infirmary — Days 3-6

The next day, Noah reported the new details to his agents again. They took note of them all.

Throughout the week, this routine would repeat. Noah would have more visions, becoming clearer each time, and giving all the details to his agents. From what they told him, the search was getting narrower. Noah's condition also improved; he no longer needed morphine, and he no longer laughed at his brother's death. It seemed like everything was coming together.

The agents showed Noah the progress they've made. Agents set aside a select few for further investigation. They shaded and marked different districts of the city. Despite the fact that good progress was being made, Noah felt it wasn't enough, like it wouldn't lead them anywhere. Something was wrong.

As Noah got off morphine, the visions of the house faded away, but the final dream was special. It was the most vivid of them all. He was there. He could walk around, look around, and explore the place. It was this night when Noah realized the truth.

It was a cabin. It was located near a lake, surrounded by lush plains and distant forests. It was far out of the city. Inside, the Dreamers probably hung out in one certain room. It had a large carpet on the floor, a ceiling light in the middle, and a table nearby with empty pizza boxes. The first level was the biggest giveaway, with a rock fireplace, wooden walls, a high ceiling and a loft above. The upstairs level didn't have much. The front of the cabin had huge windows to let in as much daylight as possible, adding to the distinct appearance of the luxurious lake house.

Eventually, the agents informed Noah that their search was coming to a conclusion. They showed him twelve images of places they marked as possible hideouts, hoping one of them would match his visions and descriptions. But Noah shook his head.

"None of them."

He asked to access the satellite map. When they let him use it, he dragged the view outside the city.

"Wait, what are you doing?"

"Last night, I saw it all. It's nowhere in the city. It was a cabin near a lake. I saw some forest too. It's far from here."

Soon, Noah found what he was looking for.

"Here!" He zoomed in.

Sure enough, the lake matched his memory, and the cabin was there too, looking real familiar. Noah felt a shiver down his spine as he was still in disbelief. Butterflies flew around his stomach as he zoomed closer. He clicked the street view, and the image almost exactly replicated what he had seen. He stepped back and put his hands on his head in shock. He also felt an urge of excitement. This must be the place.

Chapter 9

"Alright gentlemen," spoke the commander. "Here's the briefing. Team Alpha over here," he continued, gesturing to the squad to his right. "Will lead this raid. Once they bust in, they will make their arrests, and sanctions will be decided thereafter. And if they resist in any way, that's where team Bravo comes in." He gestured to the squad on his left. "They will then be authorized to use lethal force against the Dreamers and put an end to it all."

Noah raised his hand, and the commander answered, "I have a question. If we arrest them successfully, how will that help the whole situation? They could easily continue what they're doing in prison. The only reasonable punishment would be the death sentence, and that's just the same thing with extra steps."

"The sentencing isn't our matter to decide. Our only job is to capture them and bring them in. Afterwards, the federal court will decide on the punishment. Even then, we'd have to be lucky for the judge to give the death penalty. There's a chance they may not want to, or there's a chance of their mind being taken over. Which leads me to my next point."

Noah nodded.

"These Dreamers, as you all know, have some telepathic abilities beyond comprehension. They've been controlling minds, and they can do it again. Which means, even if they don't physically resist arrest, it will be counted anyway if they attempt to use their psychic power to do so. This is where Noah comes in." He gestured towards Noah.

"Huh?"

"Noah. You'll come with us. We'll keep you at a safe distance, on standby. You'll use your psychic ability to monitor the Dreamers' brain activity. *You* can detect their resistant actions where *we* can't. When you pick this up, you can give team Bravo the go. That is possible, right?"

"Hm… yeah. Got it."

I can do this, right? Surely.

The SWAT trucks roared as they drove straight through forests and plains. The team was determined to end it all. The soldiers were prepared and energized. Noah felt slightly unsure of himself. He didn't have long to train for this moment of testing. But now there was no turning back.

Huh? The SWAT's coming?

When the squad arrived, team Alpha busted through the door with their weapons and cuffs out, ready to tackle anything in their way. They searched the entire cabin until the upstairs room was found, with all five Dreamers caught in the middle of the act. Four of them, except Magnus, were panicking, frantically trying to think of a way out of this mess. Magnus hardly noticed. He was too concentrated.

"Wait... I feel something," Noah said.

"Go! Go! They're resisting! They're trying to break into the SWAT's minds!"

Team Bravo dashed into the cabin, ready to fire at will. Suddenly, the loud echo of many gunshots filled the area, and four of the Dreamers quickly died. When Magnus finally snapped out of his state, he noticed everything that had been going on. He looked at his deceased friends.

He looked at SWAT. He gave an agitated glare.

Noah had a sudden vision of the dream prison. The sky was red. The cells were open. Inmates spoke with each other, confused, relieved, and scared. No one ruled the sky. One by one, people began to disappear from the prison. The reign of terror was finally over. This was the end.

Magnus was cuffed, being escorted out of the cabin. He was staring down at the ground. He looked ashamed, but Noah could see a hidden smirk. Suddenly, his handcuffs were unlocked and fell to the ground as every single SWAT soldier started yelling and groaning. Some had their hands on their eyes. Others were staring up at the sky or flailing their heads around in an attempt to see something. Anything. Soon, they all fell to the ground unconscious. Without missing a beat.

Noah exclaimed, "What did you do?"

Magnus jerked his head to the side. He finally noticed Noah.

"*Yoouu!*" he hissed. "*You did this!*"

Quickly, he grabbed a pistol from a SWAT member and pointed it at Noah.

"Ha! What are you gonna do now? I may go to hell, but you're coming with me! I can't wait to hear your last words, you puny scoundrel!"

Noah felt *all* the shivers down his spine. He felt *all* the butterflies in his stomach. He got *all* the goosebumps. But he had to act fast.

"Listen..." Noah closed his eyes as he spoke. He began to breach Magnus' mind. "You terrorized the world... You killed many people... That includes my brother... I know you won't learn. You're rotten to the core. No possible punishment in the world could change your ill, challenged, pathetic mind."

"What was that, punk?" Magnus started to look like he was trying to develop another mental connection, but as he'd realized before, it was no use anymore. Noah was too strong.

"But let me tell you one thing." Noah took a deep breath. He focused hard. He kept calm. "In the end, everything just works out. It's funny, isn't it? One way or another, order will be restored."

"What the hell are you saying here?" His hand started to shake. He struggled to point the gun. He felt doubt grow within him.

"Playtime's over, dipshit."

Magnus' thick skull was now the direct victim of the gun. He had lost control over his own body.

Bang!

Magnus' body dropped to the ground with a satisfying thud.

For the first time in forever, Noah slept very well that night. He was strong. He was free.

Karma

The painting showed a familiar man lying under a pile of rubble. The area, ablaze like an inferno, encompassed the pile of rocks and metal bars. He had a disappointing look on his face, while people in the background were ecstatic and jubilant, laughing and cheering. The paintings finally made sense.

After half a minute of admiring the picture though, a new one appeared. The canvas slowly faded to black, and a white outline began to form. Soon, the picture came to resemble a monochrome butterfly with sharp wings and dark eyes.

Almost